KIDS' SPORTS STORIES

CHEERS FOR GYMNASTICS

by Cari Meister

illustrated by Genevieve Kote

PICTURE WINDOW BOOKS
a capstone imprint

Kids' Sports Stories is published by Picture Window Books, an imprint of Capstone.
1710 Roe Crest Drive, North Mankato, Minnesota 56003
www.capstonepub.com

Library of Congress Cataloging-in-Publication Data is available
on the Library of Congress website.
ISBN 978-1-5158-4804-2 (library binding)
ISBN 978-1-5158-5877-5 (paperback)
ISBN 978-1-5158-4805-9 (eBook PDF)

Summary: Mateo is used to being the best member of his gymnastics team. When a new boy with stronger skills joins, Mateo's jealousy threatens to knock everyone off balance right before the big Winter Challenge event.

Designer: Ted Williams

Printed in the United States of America.
PA100

TABLE OF CONTENTS

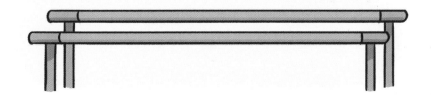

Glossary

floor—a large, springy flat surface; during the floor event, gymnasts tumble and do flips and twists

high bar—a tall piece of equipment that includes one horizontal bar on which gymnasts swing

mushroom—a short, round piece of equipment used by younger male gymnasts to build swinging and balancing skills

parallel bars—a piece of equipment that has two long, wooden bars on which gymnasts swing

rings—a piece of equipment that includes two rings hanging from a metal frame

vault—a piece of equipment that gymnasts run toward and flip over

Chapter 1
THE NEW KID

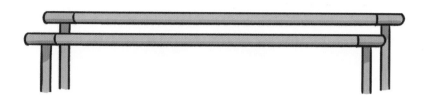

When Mateo, Greyson, and Jordan got to gymnastics practice, Coach Charlie was already standing by the gym door. A small boy stood next to him.

"Boys, this is Aaron," said Coach Charlie. "He is joining our team. He just moved here."

Jordan and Greyson smiled and said hi.

Mateo didn't say anything. He liked the team the way it was. He didn't want the new kid to wreck it.

"Let's show Aaron our warm-up," said Coach Charlie.

The boys ran in circles on the floor. They did jumping jacks and push-ups. They did forward rolls, handstands, and frog jumps. Then they stretched.

Greyson couldn't stretch very far, but he was getting better.

"I can almost reach my toes now!" he said.

"Look at me!" said Mateo, laughing. "I can lick my knees!"

"Mateo is super bendy," Jordan said to Aaron. "He can do the splits."

Later in class, the boys saw that Aaron could do the splits too. Mateo frowned.

The boys practiced the parallel bars.

They practiced swings on the high bar.

Then they did jumps on the vault.

Mateo and Aaron had the same skills.
When they got to the mushroom, though,
Aaron was stronger. He spun around the
mushroom in a full circle! None of the boys
could believe it.

"Wow, Aaron!" said Jordan. "That was
great!"

Aaron smiled. "Thanks," he said.

Mateo ran to the mushroom.

"I can do that," he said. He tried to do a circle but fell. His face turned red.

Soon Coach Charlie blew his whistle. Class was over.

"On Wednesday, we'll get ready for the Winter Challenge," he said. "Be ready to work hard!"

Chapter 2
TIME OUT

Coach Charlie explained the Winter Challenge to the boys.

"The meet is on Saturday," he said. "Each of you will compete in all six events. There will be real judges."

"Will there be ribbons?" asked Mateo. "I want all blue ribbons!"

"Yes," said Coach Charlie. "But remember, the meet is not just about what you can do. It's also about cheering on your teammates."

All the boys nodded, except Mateo.

After warming up, the boys started on floor. They practiced the first pass. It was a handstand to a forward roll, two cartwheels, and a backward roll.

"Point your toes!" Coach Charlie reminded them.

Coach Charlie showed everyone how to do the second pass. It ended with a flip.

"I can't do that last part," said Jordan.

"Me neither!" said Greyson.

"I can!" yelled Mateo. "Watch me!"

Mateo ran out on the floor.

"Watch out!" yelled Coach Charlie.

Mateo wasn't listening—or looking. He crashed right into a girl from another class.

"Mateo!" Coach Charlie said. "You have to be careful in the gym. You could really hurt someone. Take a break."

Mateo sat and watched as Aaron did
the second pass perfectly—even the flip.
Everyone cheered, except Mateo. After
10 minutes, Mateo rejoined the team.

Rings were next. Mateo did the routine well. He even landed with both feet together.

"Way to stick the landing!" Aaron said to Mateo. He put his hand up for a high five.

Mateo walked past. He didn't say anything. He didn't high-five Aaron.

Jordan whispered in Mateo's ear. "Why are you acting so weird?" Jordan asked. "Aaron's cool."

Mateo sighed. "Why does he have to be so good at everything?" he asked. "I'm supposed to be the best on this team."

"No one person makes a team, Mateo," Jordan said. "Remember what Coach said. The team's strongest when we all cheer each other on. Aaron doesn't make you weaker. He makes the team stronger!"

Mateo knew Jordan was right. He had to show he could be a good teammate.

Chapter 3

THE WINTER CHALLENGE

It was time for the Winter Challenge. The gym looked like the North Pole. Snowflakes hung from the ceiling. The judges were wearing reindeer antlers.

Mateo went first on floor. He started well, but then he tripped and fell.

The other boys cheered him on, especially Aaron. "It's OK! Finish strong!" they shouted.

When Mateo was done, he sat down and wiped away a tear. Aaron gave him a thumbs-up. Mateo gave him a small smile. Jordan and Greyson went next. Aaron went last. He looked great! Mateo clapped.

After floor, the boys did parallel bars, vault, high bar, and rings. They had some wobbles and misses. There were a couple bad landings. But the teammates whistled and cheered each other on.

"One more event," said Coach Charlie.

"Mushroom!"

Mateo went first. He took a deep breath. He placed his hands on the mushroom. *Do it, Mateo!* he said to himself. *Do it for the team!* With one big movement, he swung his legs around. Mateo made a full circle! He did it!

Coach Charlie cheered. Mateo's teammates jumped and yelled. When he finished, they ran onto the mat and put their arms around him. "Yay! That was great!" they said.

"You're the best, Mateo!" Aaron shouted.

Mateo shook his head. "No, our team's the best!" he said. "I'm sorry for being so mean to you before, Aaron. I wasn't a very good teammate."

"Thanks, Mateo," Aaron said. "We're OK."
Jordan squeezed his teammates tight. "I
knew you guys would work it out!" he said.

"Three cheers for gymnastics!"
the boys shouted.

HEALTHY EATING TIPS

Everyone should eat healthy, but especially if you play sports. Drink a lot of water and cut down on sugar. Before practice, try one of these good-for-you snacks:

- a hard-boiled egg
- celery and peanut butter
- a small turkey sandwich
- yogurt and fruit

Your muscles work hard when you play sports. After practice, refuel your body with a protein snack. Some good picks:

- a smoothie
- chocolate milk
- a protein bar
- bananas with peanut butter
- cheese and crackers

Take another look at this illustration. Only Mateo looks unhappy when Aaron shows how "bendy" he is. Jordan and Greyson cheer Aaron on.

Now pretend you are Jordan. Write an e-mail to Mateo to cheer him up. Explain why having a new teammate will be good for everyone.

ABOUT THE AUTHOR

Cari Meister is the author of more than 100 books for children, including the Fairy Hill series (Scholastic) and the Tiny series (Viking). She lives with her family in Vail, Colorado. She enjoys yoga, horseback riding, skiing, and watching her boys compete in gymnastics. You can visit her online at www.carimeister.com.

ABOUT
THE ILLUSTRATOR

Genevieve Kote is an illustrator whose lively work has appeared in popular magazines such as *American Girl* and *Nickelodeon*, children's books, comics, and newspapers. When she's not illustrating, she enjoys baking and reading at her home in Montreal, Canada. View more of her artwork at genevievekote.com.